The Adventures of Gus & Isaac

Backyard Bullies

story by
Debbie Hanlon

illustrated by
Grant Boland

Gus the seagull was deathly afraid of heights. He was terrified.

When he flew higher than the rooftop, his ears hurt, his belly felt funny, and his bill started to quiver.

So Gus didn't live on the **bluffs** with the other seagulls.
He lived on top of a red and white house.
Instead of fish, Gus ate cherries from the tree next door.

Now Gus wasn't *always* afraid of heights.

When he was just a young **gaffer**,
he fell into the ocean and landed near
a pod of Grumpback whales.
Ever since that day he'd hated flying.

And every time he peeked
over the edge of the roof
of the house he lived on,
the sidewalk
looked farther
away.

Isaac the bob-tailed cat had just moved into the red and white house that very day. He was different from the other cats – he was born without a tail.

Gus the seagull was eating cherries when Isaac came out to play in the backyard for the first time.

Isaac **coopied** down in the grass.
He sniffed the air. He perked his ears.
He shifted his eyes back and forth.
He was completely still, because
when cats stay completely still they
think that no one can see them.

Vamps the cat was a **hard ticket**, a real **cockabaloo**. He was sleeping in his backyard next to Isaac's and was having the most wonderful dreams about flying. He could feel his own smile.

Suddenly he smelled something new,
something interesting,
something without a tail.
He woke up. He stretched.
His claws came out.

Vamps
didn't like
other cats,
especially
cats without
tails.

Berg the **sleveen** cat and **Flake** the **skeet** cat were hanging around nearby.

**Vamps, Berg, and Flake crept up
on Isaac the bob-tailed cat,
but Isaac knew they were there.**

**He could smell them. He could
see their shadows in the grass.**

Those three cats were snarly and mean.
They were bullies and brazen little
brats who always picked on other cats.

Vamps nodded his head, and the
three cats pounced on Isaac.

They rolled on the ground.

They snarled and bit.

They scrawbed and they clawed.

Vamps gave Isaac a clout in the head.

POW

Gus the seagull watched the fight from the cherry tree.

He saw the three cats jump on his new neighbour, Isaac the bob-tailed cat.

Unfair and mean, he thought. He had to do something. But his belly felt funny and his bill began to quiver.

Gus closed his eyes.
He gulped down a deep breath
and swallowed.
He jumped from the cherry tree,
swooping over the fighting cats.
"Ohhhhh this is scary," he said.

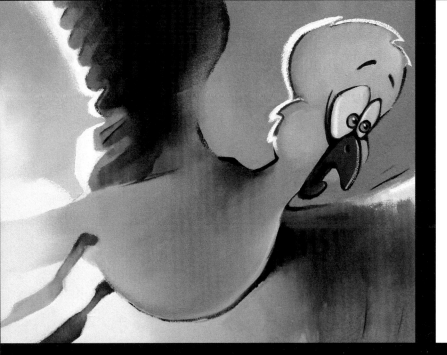

When Gus zoomed over the fight,
Isaac broke free.

He ran away as fast as he could.
The bullies were close behind.

Isaac was so afraid he was in a dwall.

Isaac ran as fast as he could up
the stairs and to the bridge.
Up from the bridge to the rail
jumped Isaac.
Up from the bridge to the rail
jumped Vamps, Berg, and Flake.

Because Isaac had no tail, he could jump higher than other cats could. From the rail he leaped all the way to the roof of his house, where Gus the seagull lived, leaving Vamps, Berg, and Flake down below.

Gus **slewed** and **skittered** away from Isaac.

"Don't be such a **scardy cat**," Isaac yelled, "I'm no bully!"

Gus turned to Isaac and said, "I'm not a scardy cat, I'm a scardy gull."

"If you're afraid, why don't you just fly away?" Isaac asked.

Gus looked sad. "I don't like flying," he said. "I'm **afeard** of heights."

Isaac knew what it was like to be afraid. Other cats were always teasing and chasing him because he was different.

"But you just flew," said Isaac.

"I did, didn't I?" said Gus. "I don't have to be afeard of flying."

They stood together and looked down at the snarling, hissing cats on Isaac's bridge.

"How will you get home?" Gus asked.

On the roof was a spudgel filled with rainwater.
"Let's give them a surprise shower," Isaac said.
Isaac put his front paws on the spudgel and pushed.
Gus put his back against the spudgel and pushed.

They pushed until the spudgel tipped over, drenching Vamps, Berg, and Flake with water.

The snarly cats ran away as fast as they could run.

Later that day, when the evening came in through
The Narrows and drew shadows on the streets,
Gus the seagull, who used to be afraid of heights,
and Isaac the bob-tailed cat sat on the rooftop.

They watched the moon rise over the water and they yarned of all the wonderful adventures they would have together.

Glossary

Afeard	Even worse than scared or afraid. Gus was really, really, really, really afraid of heights.
Gaffer	Someone young, like Gus, who is new to whatever they're doing but who is trying hard.
Bluffs	Cliffs that rise out of the ocean where seagulls normally live. Bluffs are like a high-rise apartment building for birds.
Coopied	To bend down low to the ground, like Isaac does when he is trying to be invisible.
Vamps	A pair of knitted slippers that keep your feet warm on cold floors.
Hard Ticket	Someone who is always either in trouble or about to get into trouble, like Vamps, Berg, and Flake.
Cockabaloo	A bully, like Vamps, who picks on people who are usually smaller than them.
Berg	A piece of ice that fell off an iceberg and got lost.
Sleveen	Someone young who doesn't listen to their parents or do their homework.
Flake	A place for laying out fish and letting them dry in the sun.

Scrawb	To scratch someone with your fingernails when you're angry, like the bully cats did to Isaac.
Clout	To hit someone with your fist, like when Vamps gave Isaac a clout.
Dirty Dogfish	A way of saying something bad when you are surprised without sounding like you're saying something bad.
In a Dwall	When you're confused and aren't sure what to do next or where to go.
Bridge	The steps leading up to your house or the back deck on your house.
Slewed	To tip to one side like you're walking in a really strong windstorm.
Skittered	To move your feet very fast as you walk like a spider.
Scardy Cat	Someone who is afraid of something that they don't need to be afraid of, like Gus who was afraid of flying.
Spudgel	A square wooden bucket with a handle used for scooping water out of a boat so it doesn't sink.
Yarned	To tell stories to your friends about things you're going to do together, like Gus and Isaac do.

About the
Author

Debbie is an elected city councillor, a national and international columnist, and an award-winning business-woman. She is the mom of three children who finally left home, giving her time to write about Gus and Isaac. Debbie currently lives in St. John's with her husband and her bob-tailed cat named Isaac.

www.debbiehanlonconnection.com

Visit Gus & Isaac online

About the Illustrator

Grant has held multiple solo and group exhibitions. He has been awarded the CBC Emerging Artist of the Year award as well as two Elizabeth Greenshields awards for painting. Grant and his three-year-old son Jack worked on the images in this book together. Jack was wondering if Gus pooped on the whales.

www.grantboland.net

www.gusandisaac.com

Dedicated to baby James,
the very first of the next generation.

Thank you to my wonderful
husband, Oral Mews, who continues
to make all my dreams come true.

Debbie Hanlon

Dedicated to my son, Jack, who
is every inch a Roosterfish and
continues to make all of me smile.

Grant Boland

Library and Archives Canada Cataloguing in Publication

Hanlon, Debbie, 1965-
The Adventures of Gus & Isaac / Debbie Hanlon ; Grant Boland, illustrator.
ISBN 978-1-55081-363-0
I. Boland, Grant, 1972- II. Title. III. Title: Adventures of Gus & Isaac.
PS8615.A5545A68 2011   jC813'.6   C2011-906013-2

Breakwater Books acknowledges the support of the Canada Council for the Arts which last year invested $20.1 million in writing and publishing throughout Canada. We acknowledge the Government of Canada through the Canada Book Fund and the Government of Newfoundland and Labrador through the Department of Tourism, Culture and Recreation for our publishing activities.

 Canada Council for the Arts   Conseil des Arts du Canada   Canada   Newfoundland Labrador

Printed and bound in Canada

 Breakwater Books is committed to choosing papers and materials for our books that help to protect our environment. To this end, this book is printed on a recycled paper that is certified by the Forest Stewardship Council of Canada. **www.breakwaterbooks.com**